SUPER RABBIT BOY'S TEAM-UP TROUBLE!

READ MORE
PRESS START!
BOOKS!

1

2

3

4

5

6

7

8

9

10

11

MORE BOOKS COMING SOON!

PRESS START!

SUPER RABBIT BOY'S TEAM-UP TROUBLE!

THOMAS FLINTHAM

SCHOLASTIC INC.

FOR MY SUPER SISTER, SALLY

Copyright © 2021 by Thomas Flintham

All rights reserved. Published by Scholastic Inc., *Publishers since 1920.* SCHOLASTIC, BRANCHES, and associated logos are trademarks and/or registered trademarks of Scholastic Inc.

The publisher does not have any control over and does not assume any responsibility for author or third-party websites or their content.

No part of this publication may be reproduced, stored in a retrieval system, or transmitted in any form or by any means, electronic, mechanical, photocopying, recording, or otherwise, without written permission of the publisher. For information regarding permission, write to Scholastic Inc., Attention: Permissions Department, 557 Broadway, New York, NY 10012.

This book is a work of fiction. Names, characters, places, and incidents are either the product of the author's imagination or are used fictitiously, and any resemblance to actual persons, living or dead, business establishments, events, or locales is entirely coincidental.

Library of Congress Cataloging-in-Publication Data

Names: Flintham, Thomas, author, illustrator.
Title: Super Rabbit Boy's team-up trouble! / Thomas Flintham.
Description: First edition. | New York : Branches/Scholastic Inc., 2021. |
Series: Press start! ; 10 | Summary: When King Viking, Miss Business, and their henchmen team up to cause trouble, Super Rabbit Boy and Mega Mole Girl also join forces, but will they be able to work together to save the world?
Identifiers: LCCN 2020024281 (print) | LCCN 2020024282 (ebook) | ISBN 9781338568998 (paperback) | ISBN 9781338569001 (library binding) | ISBN 9781338569018 (ebook)
Subjects: CYAC: Superheroes—Fiction. | Supervillains—Fiction. | Animals—Fiction. | Video games—Fiction.
Classification: LCC PZ7.1.F585 Svg 2021 (print) | LCC PZ7.1.F585 (ebook | DDC [Fic]—dc23
LC record available at https://lccn.loc.gov/2020024281
LC ebook record available at https://lccn.loc.gov/2020024282

10 9 8 7 6 5 4 3 2   21 22 23 24 25

Printed in the U.S.A.   40
First edition, April 2021
Edited by Katie Carella and Alli Brydon
Book design by Maria Mercado

TABLE OF CONTENTS

One rainy day at Carrot Castle, Super Rabbit Boy is practicing his Super Jumps. Suddenly, the ground starts to shake!

Super Rabbit Boy runs inside to check his Super Trouble Detector. It shows him where trouble might be happening nearby.

Super Rabbit Boy bounces over to the Ultra Cave.

But when he arrives, there is no sign of trouble.

Maybe something happened inside?

The ground shifts below Super Rabbit Boy.
He almost tumbles over!

It's Mega Mole Girl!

ONE RAINY DAY LONG AGO, MOLE GIRL SAVED A WORM'S LIFE.

BUT THE WORM WAS NO ORDINARY WORM. IT WAS THE MEGA MAGIC WORM! TO SAY THANKS, IT GAVE MOLE GIRL SOME OF ITS POWERS.

2 DOUBLE TROUBLE

Super Rabbit Boy and Mega Mole Girl rush inside the cave. They find Cave Explorer Kirk. He is trapped under a rock.

13

The brave heroes leap into the tunnel!

Super Rabbit Boy and Mega Mole Girl
land in a dark cavern.

Super Rabbit Boy uses his Super Jump.

Mega Mole Girl uses her Super Digging Power.

They enter another cavern. There are so many tunnels.

Clive dashes toward another tunnel.

The robots surround Mega Mole Girl and Super Rabbit Boy.

The heroes jump into action! Super Rabbit Boy bounces from robot to robot. They fall to pieces.

Mega Mole Girl digs holes underneath other robots. They get stuck!

Super Rabbit Boy bounces on Mega Mole Girl's head.

Then Mega Mole Girl digs a hole underneath Super Rabbit Boy.

The two heroes have almost caught up with Clive.

Just then, Clive jumps into a Robo-Boss! He's ready to battle.

I got a promotion! I'm an end-of-level boss now!

4 TEAM-UP TROUBLES

Super Rabbit Boy jumps toward Clive and the Robo-Boss.

23

But before Super Rabbit Boy can strike, the ground opens. Mega Mole Girl has dug a hole underneath the Robo-Boss.

The Robo-Boss tries to climb out of the hole. But Super Rabbit Boy bounces right on top of it with his Super Jump.

Clive and the Robo-Boss are defeated! But as the Robo-Boss crashes down into the hole, it almost lands on Mega Mole Girl!

Suddenly, everything starts to shake. It's another earthquake!

5 FALLING DOWN AND OUT

The heroes find another deep, dark tunnel.

Super Rabbit Boy and Mega Mole Girl come out the other side. They are in an empty, old underground city!

Super Rabbit Boy bounces through the city.

Hey! Wait for me!

Super Rabbit Boy bounces fast from rooftop to rooftop. Mega Mole Girl falls behind.

We're supposed to be working together!

That's not fair! I can't jump like you.

That's not my fault.

Soon, Super Rabbit Boy finds his path blocked by a giant fence.

He jumps down to the ground and finds Mega Mole Girl on the other side.

Super Rabbit Boy finds a route around the fence. He finally catches up with Mega Mole Girl.

You could have helped me back there!

You left me behind, so I didn't think you needed my help!

If you two want to fight, you should fight ME instead!

Another of Miss Business's personal assistants steps forward. She is inside another Robo-Boss!

I'm Senior Support Supervisor Susan.

Miss Business paid King Viking lots of money to build this Robo-Boss. It is strong!

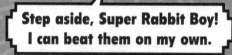

Step aside, Super Rabbit Boy! I can beat them on my own.

Me, too! I don't need your help.

Can Super Rabbit Boy beat Susan and the Robo-Boss on his own?

The battle begins! Mega Mole Girl digs lots of pits and tunnels.

Super Rabbit Boy leaps onto the rooftops. Using his Super Jump, he sends bricks and stones flying toward the Robo-Boss.

The Robo-Boss is under attack from above <u>and</u> below. It is struggling to avoid the falling stones and the holes in the ground at the same time.

The Robo-Boss leaps over a hole right into the path of a falling stone.

The stone knocks the Robo-Boss into the hole.

Susan and the Robo-Boss are defeated!

Another earthquake shakes the city.

Super Rabbit Boy and Mega Mole Girl find another tunnel. It leads deeper underground.

I'll find the meanies and put a stop to this.

No, I'll stop them!

They pop out the other side — into a cavern filled with hot lava.

Super Rabbit Boy and Mega Mole Girl set off in different directions. Their team-up has come to an end.

Super Rabbit Boy bounces from rock to rock. He avoids the lava.

He lands on a rock. It starts to sink!

Super Rabbit Boy quickly leaps to another rock. But now he has nowhere to go!

Meanwhile, Mega Mole Girl digs a tunnel below the lava.

But lava starts pouring inside it!

She digs up and away from the lava.

Mega Mole Girl jumps out of her tunnel.

She is surrounded by lava.
And she has nowhere to go!

Oh dear.

47

The heroes are still surrounded by lava.

Suddenly, a giant robot hand swoops
down. It grabs Mega Mole Girl!

It's another personal assistant in a Robo-Boss. The Robo-Boss hangs from the storm clouds.

The Robo-Boss tries to grab Super Rabbit Boy.

Super Rabbit Boy hops up. Mega Mole Girl frees herself from the robot's grip.

With Mega Mole Girl on his back, Super
Rabbit Boy leaps from the Robo-Boss onto a
nearby cliff.

The Robo-Boss climbs onto the cliff.

Super Rabbit Boy is ready to hop away.
But Mega Mole Girl has a different plan.

She digs down through the cliff.

As she does this, the edge of the cliff falls into the lava. It takes the Robo-Boss with it!

Miss Business will fire me when she hears about this.

Super Rabbit Boy and Mega Mole Girl don't have time to celebrate. The ground shakes again.

9 THROUGH THE ULTRA DOOR

The heroes finally spot King Viking and Miss Business. The Mega Diggerbot is digging deeper.

Stop right there!

The Ultra Door opens a portal to the surface. It leads to King Viking's Factory!

The robots that Miss Business ordered come running through the portal.

Robots, keep them busy while we grab the Ultra Diamond!

BEEP!

BOOP!

Super Rabbit Boy and Mega Mole Girl know what to do.

Together, we can beat all these robots!

Mega Mole Girl digs around the robots, trapping them all in one spot.

Then Super Rabbit Boy bounces from robot to robot and smashes them to pieces.

Mega Mole Girl and Super Rabbit Boy
have defeated the robots!

The meanies have dug all the way to the
center of the planet!

The heroes finally reach the planet's core.

King Viking and Miss Business are about to grab the Ultra Diamond!

King Viking tugs on the Ultra Diamond, trying to loosen it.

The meanies pull in opposite directions. The Ultra Diamond is very hard to get out.

Before the meanies can grab the Ultra Diamond, they start to fall! They were so busy arguing, they didn't notice Mega Mole Girl digging below them.

King Viking and Miss Business fall in and zoom down Mega Mole Girl's tunnel!

When the villains fly out the other end of the tunnel, Super Rabbit Boy is ready. He is waiting — with the Ultra Door wide open!

The meanies fly through the Ultra Door and warp back to the surface.

Then Super Rabbit Boy and Mega Mole Girl smash the Ultra Door so the meanies can't come back through it.

THOMAS FLINTHAM

has always loved to draw and tell stories, and now that is his job! He grew up in Lincoln, England, and studied illustration in Camberwell, London. He lives by the sea with his wife, Bethany, in Cornwall.

Thomas is the creator of THOMAS FLINTHAM'S BOOK OF MAZES AND PUZZLES and many other books for kids. PRESS START! is his first early chapter book series.

Mega Diggerbot is very tired after digging down to the planet's core. The robot is fast asleep and dreaming about the search for the Ultra Diamond. Can you find the Ultra Diamond hidden in this pattern?

PRESS START!

How much do you know about
SUPER RABBIT BOY'S
TEAM-UP TROUBLE!

The ground shakes on pages 2, 26, 39, and 56. What keeps making the ground shake? (Hint: Reread page 13!)

When Super Rabbit Boy and Mega Mole Girl reach the Ultra Cave, they meet Cave Explorer Kirk. What does he tell them?

How did Mega Mole Girl get her superpower? Retell her backstory in your own words.

Three meanies work for Miss Business: Executive Team Leader Clive, Senior Support Supervisor Susan, and Deputy Office Manager Roger. Why do you think the author gave Miss Business's meanies these names?

The Ultra Diamond keeps the world safe. How do you think its power works? Draw a picture of the Ultra Diamond and show how it keeps the world safe.

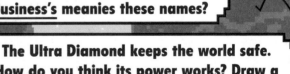